Songbird's Lullaby: Whispers of Elderwood

Mrigendra Bharti

Published by Sellbrochure Vymish Entertainment, 2024.

This is a work of fiction. Similarities to real people, places, or events are entirely coincidental.

SONGBIRD'S LULLABY: WHISPERS OF ELDERWOOD

First edition. June 21, 2024.

Copyright © 2024 Mrigendra Bharti.

ISBN: 979-8227624635

Written by Mrigendra Bharti.

Table of Contents

Preface

Welcome, dear reader, to the enchanting realm of Elderwood, a village nestled amidst verdant hills and embraced by the whispering embrace of the ancient Whispering Woods. Here, nature's rhythms pulse in harmony with the lives of its inhabitants, their existence intertwined with the secrets and wonders that lie hidden within the forest's depths.

At the heart of Elderwood stands the majestic banyan tree, its gnarled branches reaching towards the heavens, its roots burrowing deep into the earth's embrace. This venerable sentinel serves as a conduit for the whispers, a symphony of nature's voices that guide and nurture the village's inhabitants.

Among them is Kiran, a young woman with eyes the color of moss and a spirit as wild as the wind. Kiran possesses an uncanny understanding of the whispers, her senses attuned to the subtle nuances of the forest's language. She spends her days exploring the tangled depths of the Whispering Woods, deciphering the secrets that the rustling leaves and gurgling streams impart.

One crisp morning, an unsettling silence descends upon Elderwood, the familiar whispers replaced by an ominous stillness. Unease grips Kiran's heart as she ventures into the woods, the vibrant foliage shrouded in an unnatural hush. The air crackles with an impending sense of doom.

Deep within the forest's embrace, she stumbles upon a horrifying sight. Twisted, blighted creatures, their forms a grotesque mockery of nature, ravage the forest floor. These are the harbingers of the Blight, a malevolent force that threatens to extinguish all life, casting a shadow of despair over Elderwood.

Panic gnaws at Kiran, but she knows she must act. She rushes to warn Elder Kaia, the village's revered leader, a woman whose wisdom is as deep as the roots of the banyan tree. Together, they confront the grim reality of the Blight's resurgence, their hearts heavy with the weight of responsibility.

Fear grips the villagers, their once peaceful existence shattered by the Blight's insidious presence. But amidst the terror, a flicker of defiance sparks in Kiran's eyes. She refuses to surrender to this encroaching darkness.

The whispers, faint but persistent, tug at her mind, guiding her towards a glimmer of hope. They speak of a hidden guardian, a protector of the forest who holds the key to repelling the Blight. Kiran feels a surge of determination. If they can find this guardian, they might yet have a chance to save their beloved Elderwood.

With Elder Kaia's blessings, Kiran embarks on a perilous quest, accompanied by Rohan, a skilled hunter known for his unwavering loyalty and sharp aim. Together, they plunge deeper into the Whispering Woods, the whispers intensifying, forming a disjointed, urgent melody.

The forest, once familiar and comforting, transforms into a labyrinth of danger. Giant, diseased vines lash out at them, and grotesque creatures spawned from the Blight lurk in the shadows. Kiran's understanding of nature, honed over years of exploration, becomes their only shield. She learns to anticipate the Blight's movements, using the whispers to guide them towards hidden paths and secret clearings.

One twilight, they stumble upon a clearing bathed in an eerie green glow. In its center stands a gnarled, ancient tree, its twisted branches clawing at the sky. The air crackles with energy, and the whispers converge into a single, chilling voice: "Welcome, foolish trespassers. The forest belongs to the Blight now."

Emerging from the shadows is a monstrous entity, a culmination of the Blight's corrupting essence. It resembles a grotesque amalgamation of Blight creatures, its eyes burning with an unholy light. Fear threatens to paralyze them, but Kiran steeled her resolve. This was the guardian they sought, twisted by the Blight's darkness.

Desperate to break the entity's hold on the guardian, Kiran channels the whispers, focusing on the underlying rhythm, the melody beneath the chaos. Visions flood her mind – a legend of a forgotten spring, a wellspring of life hidden deep within the forest, capable of purifying corruption and restoring balance.

A desperate plan takes root. They could lure the entity away from the clearing, giving them a chance to find the wellspring. The battle was fierce, a desperate dance between human ingenuity and unyielding corruption. Kiran and Rohan fought with a ferocity fueled by their love for their home and their unwavering conviction to save it.

Finally, with a well-placed arrow from Rohan infused with Elder Kaia's blessed herbs, they managed to distract the corrupted guardian. Kiran seized the opportunity, following the whispers' guidance, to weave through a hidden passage within the ancient tree.

The passage led to a hidden cavern, pulsating with an ethereal light emanating from strange, bioluminescent plants. In the center stood a shimmering pool

Prologue:

The wind whispered secrets through the ancient boughs of the Whispering Woods. Not the playful chirps and murmurs Kiran had grown accustomed to, but a chilling symphony of warning and despair. A suffocating silence had descended upon Elderwood, the village nestled within the forest's embrace. The once vibrant canopy hung heavy and oppressive, casting the forest floor in an unsettling gloom.

Kiran, her heart pounding a frantic rhythm against her ribs, ventured deeper. The whispers, once her constant companions, seemed to recoil from her approach, leaving her adrift in a sea of uncertainty. Years spent exploring the woods had honed her senses, and the unnatural stillness screamed of danger.

She stumbled upon a clearing, its beauty marred by a horrifying sight. Twisted, grotesque creatures, their forms a mockery of nature, ravaged the once pristine foliage. These were the Blight, harbingers of destruction whispered about in hushed tones by the elders. Panic threatened to overwhelm her, but Kiran steeled herself. Elderwood needed her.

Memories surfaced – stories from her childhood, tales spun fireside by her grandmother, tales of a time when the Blight threatened to consume the world. Tales of a hidden wellspring, a reservoir of life energy capable of cleansing the corruption. Hope, fragile but persistent, flickered within her.

Suddenly, the air shimmered and a figure emerged from the warped shadows. Tall and imposing, clad in rusted armor etched with strange symbols, it exuded an aura of malevolent power. A chilling voice echoed in her mind, devoid of warmth or kindness: "The whispers serve no purpose now. This forest belongs to darkness."

Fear threatened to consume her, but Kiran stood her ground. This wasn't just some Blight creature; it was a guardian, a protector corrupted by the darkness. The whispers, though faint, began to coalesce, a desperate plea for help.

A vision flickered in Kiran's mind – a hidden chamber deep within the Whispering Woods, pulsating with an ethereal light. The Wellspring. With newfound determination, she channeled the whispers, weaving them into a plan. The creature, distracted by a flicker of movement in the distance, turned its back.

This was her chance. Kiran darted forward, her heart pounding a frantic rhythm against her ribs. The whispers, now a desperate chorus, guided her through a hidden passage, a secret entrance veiled by cascading vines. The Blight's guardian roared in frustration, the sound echoing through the woods, but it was too late. Kiran had vanished into the heart of the forest, on a desperate quest to find the wellspring and restore balance to the Whispering Woods.

About Sellbrochure Vymish Entertainment

Sellbrochure Vymish Entertainment, recognized as India's largest book publishing company, has made significant strides in ensuring its extensive collection of books reaches audiences across the global market. This rapid expansion is a testament to the company's dedication to disseminating knowledge and literature far beyond national borders. Central to its success is its affiliation with InkWhirl Media Networks, a reputable entity in the media and publication industry known for its innovative and strategic approaches. Within this network, InkWhirl Publication LLC operates as a vital division, further enhancing the company's capabilities and reach in the international market.

The visionary behind this enterprise is Mrigendra Bharti, the founder of Sellbrochure Vymish Entertainment. His foresight and passion for the literary world have been instrumental in steering the company towards remarkable growth and recognition. Under his leadership, Sellbrochure Vymish Entertainment has not only expanded its catalog but also established a strong presence in both domestic and international markets. Mrigendra Bharti's commitment to excellence and innovation has been a driving force in the company's journey, ensuring that it stays ahead of industry trends and meets the evolving needs of readers worldwide.

Sellbrochure Vymish Entertainment operates under the robust support of its parental organization, Mrigendra Bharti Group InfoTech. This affiliation provides the necessary resources and strategic guidance, enabling the publishing company to undertake ambitious projects and explore new markets. Mrigendra Bharti Group InfoTech's extensive experience in technology and information services has been a valuable asset, allowing Sellbrochure Vymish Entertainment to integrate advanced digital solutions in its operations, thereby enhancing its distribution capabilities and reader engagement.

Through relentless efforts and a commitment to quality, Sellbrochure Vymish Entertainment continues to break barriers and expand the reach of Indian literature globally. The company's diverse portfolio includes a wide range of genres, catering to different age groups and interests, thereby fostering a rich and inclusive reading culture. As it continues to innovate and grow, Sellbrochure Vymish Entertainment remains dedicated to its mission of making literature accessible to all, contributing significantly to the global literary landscape.

Connect With Mrigendra,
Thank you very much for choosing this book.
You can also connect with me on Instagram,
https://www.instagram.com/i_mrigendrabharti.official
With Love,
Mrigendra Bharti

Introduction;
Songbird's Lullaby:
Whispers of
Elderwood

The wind whispered secrets through the ancient boughs of the Whispering Woods. Not the playful chirps and murmurs Kiran had grown accustomed to, but a chilling symphony of warning and despair. A suffocating silence had descended upon Elderwood, the village nestled within the forest's embrace. The once vibrant canopy hung heavy and oppressive, casting the forest floor in an unsettling gloom.

Kiran, her heart pounding a frantic rhythm against her ribs, ventured deeper. The whispers, once her constant companions, seemed to recoil from her approach, leaving her adrift in a sea of uncertainty. Years spent exploring the woods had honed her senses, and the unnatural stillness screamed of danger.

She stumbled upon a clearing, its beauty marred by a horrifying sight. Twisted, grotesque creatures, their forms a mockery of nature, ravaged the once pristine foliage. These were the Blight, harbingers of destruction whispered about in hushed tones by the elders. They resembled thorny, gnarled vines given malevolent life, their eyes glowing with an unnatural green light.

Panic threatened to overwhelm her, but Kiran steeled herself. Elderwood needed her.

Memories surfaced – stories from her childhood, tales spun fireside by her grandmother, of a time when the Blight threatened to consume the world. Tales of a hidden wellspring, a reservoir of life energy capable of cleansing the corruption. Hope, fragile but persistent, flickered within her.

Suddenly, the air shimmered and a figure emerged from the warped shadows. Tall and imposing, clad in rusted armor etched with strange symbols, it exuded an aura of malevolent power. A chilling voice echoed in her mind, devoid of warmth or kindness: "The whispers serve no purpose now. This forest belongs to darkness."

Fear threatened to consume her, but Kiran stood her ground. This wasn't just some Blight creature; it was a guardian, a protector corrupted by the darkness. The whispers, though faint, began to coalesce, a desperate plea for help.

A vision flickered in Kiran's mind – a hidden chamber deep within the Whispering Woods, pulsating with an ethereal light. The Wellspring. With newfound determination, she channeled the whispers, weaving them into a plan. The creature, distracted by a flicker of movement in the distance, turned its back.

This was her chance. Kiran darted forward, her heart pounding a frantic rhythm against her ribs. The whispers, now a desperate chorus, guided her through a hidden passage, a secret entrance veiled by cascading vines. The Blight's guardian roared in frustration, the sound echoing through the woods, but it was too late. Kiran had vanished into the heart of the forest, on a desperate quest to find the wellspring and restore balance to the Whispering Woods.

Back in Elderwood

Elder Kaia, a woman whose wisdom was as deep as the roots of the banyan tree at the village center, paced anxiously. Kiran's absence gnawed at her. News of the Blight's resurgence had spread fear throughout the village, but Kiran's disappearance amplified their anxieties.

Elder Kaia closed her eyes, focusing on the faint tendrils of the whispers that still reached her. Distorted and fractured, they spoke of a struggle, of a desperate plea for the wellspring. Relief washed over her – Kiran was alive, and she knew of the legend.

A young man with sharp eyes and a determined jawline burst into the clearing. Rohan, Kiran's childhood friend and a skilled hunter, had been searching for her. "Elder Kaia," he said, his voice tight with worry, "I can't find Kiran anywhere."

"Patience, Rohan," Elder Kaia soothed, placing a wrinkled hand on his shoulder. "Kiran is strong and resourceful. She wouldn't go off without a reason." She relayed the fragmented messages from the whispers, the hope flickering within them.

Rohan's eyes widened. "The Wellspring," he whispered, a flicker of understanding dawning on him. "It's just a legend, isn't it?"

Elder Kaia shook her head. "It's more than a legend, Rohan. It's a desperate hope. The whispers are urging us to find it."

Rohan glanced outside, at the oppressive silence of the woods. "Then we find it," he declared, his resolve hardening. "Kiran needs our help, and so does Elderwood."

With Elder Kaia's blessing, Rohan set out, the whispers leading him towards the clearing Kiran had stumbled upon. He found the remnants of the battle, the Blight creatures slain by arrows infused with Elder Kaia's blessed herbs. He discovered the hidden passage, a feat that would have been impossible without the whispers' guidance.

Following the Songbird's Lullaby

Kiran navigated through the hidden passage, The hidden passage, revealed by the whispers, twisted and turned like the gnarled roots of the ancient trees. Kiran crawled and squeezed through narrow openings, her heart pounding with exertion. The air grew cooler, damp, and heavy with the scent of moss and decaying leaves. Finally, the passage opened into a vast cavern.

An ethereal glow emanated from the cavern walls, pulsing with a soft, bioluminescent light. Glowing fungi and bioluminescent plants adorned the cavern walls, casting strange, swirling shadows on the cave floor. In the center, nestled between crystalline formations, lay a shimmering pool of water. This was it – the Wellspring.

As Kiran approached, the whispers solidified, forming a clear melody – a songbird's lullaby. It was a melody of life, purity, and hope, a stark contrast to the chilling silence that had gripped the forest. The water shimmered with an inner light, radiating a wave of peaceful energy that washed over Kiran, calming her racing heart.

Suddenly, a voice echoed through the cavern – deep, guttural, and infused with malice. "So, a curious little trespasser has stumbled upon the Wellspring."

Kiran whirled around to find the Blight guardian towering behind her, his rusted armor glinting in the cavern's glow. The corrupted energy radiating from him filled the air with a sense of oppressive darkness.

"The whispers have guided you well," the Blight guardian rasped, his voice like dry leaves crunching underfoot. "But you will not leave here alive. These waters will now be corrupted, their life force twisted to serve my master!"

Fear threatened to cripple Kiran, but she remembered Elderwood, its peaceful inhabitants now facing the Blight's wrath. She couldn't let them down. Focusing on the songbird's lullaby resonating within the cavern, Kiran reached out with her mind, trying to understand the whispers better.

Visions flooded her – intricate patterns swirling around the Wellspring, symbols etched onto the cavern walls mimicking the patterns. The whispers grew clearer, a desperate plea for her to activate the Wellspring's true potential.

With newfound resolve, Kiran traced the symbols on the wall with her fingers, replicating the patterns she saw in her vision. The cave pulsed with energy, the glowing plants intensifying their light. The water in the Wellspring churned, and a pillar of pure white light erupted from its depths, pushing back the Blight guardian's darkness.

The guardian roared in pain and fury, blinded by the light. He lashed out with claws of twisted metal, but the light deflected him. Kiran, strengthened by the wellspring's energy, felt a surge of power. This wasn't just a source of life – it was a weapon against the Blight.

She focused the light towards the Blight guardian, channeling the songbird's lullaby through the water. As the light bathed him, the corruption began to recede. The rusted armor crumbled, revealing a once-noble warrior beneath. His eyes, no longer glowing with malice, shimmered with confusion and dawning realization.

"What... what have I become?" the warrior rasped, his voice weak.

Kiran lowered her hand, the light fading. Relief flooded her as the whispers calmed, returning to their familiar melody. "You were a protector, a guardian," she said, her voice filled with hope. "But the Blight corrupted you."

The warrior looked at her, a flicker of recognition in his eyes. "The whispers... the forest... they called me." Shame filled his voice. "But the darkness... it twisted my purpose."

"There's still time," Kiran declared, a newfound confidence in her voice. "The Wellspring can help you fight it."

As the warrior knelt before the Wellspring, Kiran realized this was just the beginning. The Blight might be momentarily repelled, but the source of its corruption remained an unknown threat. The warrior, once a protector, could become a powerful ally.

Together, they could follow the whispers deeper into the heart of the Blight, unraveling its secrets and finding the source of its corruption to restore balance to the Whispering Woods. But first, they had to return to Elderwood, warn the villagers of the ongoing threat, and prepare for the fight to come.

Kiran and the warrior emerged from the cavern, the songbird's lullaby echoing in their ears, a melody of hope and a promise of a new beginning. The whispers, once silenced by fear, had returned, stronger than ever, guiding them towards their destiny. The battle for Elderwood, for the Whispering Woods, had just begun.

Chapter 1: The Hidden Door

Kiran, a wisp of a girl with eyes that mirrored the endless summer sky, was never quite present in the bustling heart of her small village. Her head perpetually hovered in the clouds, conjuring fantastical worlds where castles shimmered on mountaintops and friendly dragons soared across lavender skies. Even the rhythmic clanging of the blacksmith's hammer, a constant background score to village life, couldn't penetrate the dreamy haze that surrounded her.

One lazy afternoon, as the sun dipped below the mango orchard, casting long shadows across the dusty path, Kiran found herself drawn to the outskirts of the village. Here, nestled amidst gnarled banyan trees and whispering wild grass, stood the remnants of an old fort, its once-proud walls now crumbling testaments to the passage of time. The villagers whispered tales of a glorious past, of battles fought and won, but for Kiran, it was a place of forgotten stories, waiting to be unraveled.

Today, an unusual stillness hung in the air. The usual cacophony of crickets and chirping birds was replaced by an unsettling silence. Kiran, ever the explorer, felt a thrill course through her. Ignoring the prickle of unease at the back of her neck, she ventured deeper into the fort's ruins. Sunlight barely pierced the thick canopy of leaves overhead, casting an eerie glow on the moss-covered stones.

Suddenly, a twig snapped beneath her foot. Kiran whirled around, her heart hammering against her ribs. A flash of movement caught her eye – a blur of brown fur disappearing behind a crumbling wall. Relief washed over her – it was just Raju, the village prankster, no doubt up to his usual mischief.

Raju, Kiran's best friend since childhood, was her polar opposite. A whirlwind of boundless energy and a mischievous grin that could melt even the sternest elder's heart, he was the grounding force in Kiran's world of daydreams. The moment he emerged from his hiding place, a sheepish grin plastered on his face, Kiran's apprehension melted away.

"Scared you, did I?" he chuckled, his dark eyes twinkling.

Kiran swatted him playfully on the arm. "You scared the living daylights out of me! What are you even doing here?"

Raju shrugged, his grin fading slightly. "Same as you, I guess. Exploring."

They wandered deeper into the ruins, the silence broken only by the soft crunch of fallen leaves under their feet. The air grew thick with the scent of damp earth and decaying leaves, a melancholic reminder of the fort's forgotten glory. As they rounded a corner, a glint of metal caught Kiran's eye. Brushing aside a curtain of vines, they stumbled upon a hidden doorway, almost seamlessly embedded into the wall.

The doorway was small and arched, crafted from a dark, polished wood that seemed to gleam faintly in the dim light. Intricate carvings adorned its surface, depicting strange symbols that swirled and danced before Kiran's eyes. An undeniable pull emanated from the doorway, a whisper of something ancient and unknown.

Kiran's breath hitched in her throat. A shiver danced down her spine, both exhilarating and terrifying. This wasn't just an old doorway; it was a portal to somewhere else, somewhere hidden and mysterious.

Raju, usually fearless, hesitated for a moment, his brow furrowed in concern. He looked at Kiran, his apprehension mirrored in her wide eyes. Yet, a spark of curiosity, a yearning for adventure, flickered in both their gazes.

"What do you think is in there?" Raju's voice was barely a whisper.

Kiran swallowed hard. "I don't know," she admitted, her voice trembling slightly, "but I have a feeling we're about to find out."

The weight of the ancient door creaked in protest as Kiran and Raju pushed against it, its aged hinges groaning like the weary bones of an old man. A wave of stale air, thick with the scent of dust and something more metallic, rushed out, sending a shiver down their spines.

Kiran, her heart pounding a frantic rhythm against her ribs, peeked through the narrow opening. Sunlight, slanting through cracks in the wall on the other side, illuminated a passage that plunged into darkness. The air shimmered with an unnatural heat, distorting the outlines of the rough-hewn stones that formed the walls.

Raju, ever the pragmatist, placed a hand on Kiran's shoulder, his touch grounding her soaring imagination. "Are you sure about this?" he asked, his voice barely a whisper in the oppressive silence.

Kiran met his gaze, a spark of determination replacing the flicker of fear. "There's only one way to find out," she replied, her voice surprisingly steady. Taking a deep breath, she squeezed his hand reassuringly. "We'll face it together, like always."

A smile, hesitant at first but growing wider with each passing moment, stretched across Raju's face. The familiar warmth of their camaraderie, a bond forged through countless childhood adventures, chased away the lingering shadows of doubt. With a silent nod, they stepped through the doorway, leaving behind the familiar world bathed in the golden glow of the setting sun.

The passage was narrow and uneven, forcing them to walk single file. The air grew thicker, the metallic tang more pronounced. An unsettling silence pressed down on them, broken only by the soft scrape of their sandals against the rough stone floor. Kiran, her senses on high alert, scanned the darkness ahead, searching for any sign of what lay hidden beyond the veil of shadows.

Suddenly, a flicker of movement caught her eye. A small, luminous orb, like a firefly trapped in a spider's web, danced erratically in the distance. Kiran gasped, her hand instinctively reaching for Raju's arm. He squeezed her hand back, a silent reassurance in the face of the unknown.

As they cautiously ventured deeper, the passage opened into a vast cavern. The sight that greeted them stole their breath away. Crystal formations, sparkling like a million captured stars, lined the cavern walls, casting an ethereal glow that illuminated the fantastical scene before them. Strange, bioluminescent plants dotted the cavern floor, their otherworldly luminescence painting the cavern in an ever-shifting kaleidoscope of colors.

In the center of the cavern, a magnificent tree unlike any they had ever seen stood tall. Its bark shimmered with an otherworldly silver sheen, and its leaves, resembling polished emeralds, emitted a soft, pulsating light. Wisps of mist swirled around its base, adding to the air of mystery that permeated the cavern.

Kiran and Raju stood transfixed, speechless in the face of this breathtaking spectacle. It was as if they had stumbled upon a forgotten corner of a dream, a place where reality shimmered at the edges of fantasy. A sense of wonder, tinged with a hint of trepidation, washed over them. This hidden world, untouched by time, pulsed with an ancient energy that sent shivers down their spines.

Breaking the spell, a soft chirping sound echoed through the cavern. Kiran whirled around, her heart hammering against her ribs. A small, winged creature, no bigger than her hand, fluttered towards them. Its body resembled a hummingbird, but its wings shimmered with iridescent scales that seemed to catch the very essence of the cavern's luminescence.

The creature hovered in front of them, its large, intelligent eyes gazing at them curiously. Kiran felt a strange sense of connection with the creature, a feeling of peace and welcome that soothed the prickling fear at the edges of her mind. Raju, ever cautious, watched the creature with a wary eye, his hand instinctively reaching for the slingshot nestled in his pocket.

As the creature tilted its head, a soft trill escaped its throat, a sound that seemed to resonate deep within Kiran's soul. A strange certainty bloomed within her – this creature wasn't a threat, but a guide, a sentinel of this hidden world. Tentatively, she reached out a hand, her fingers trembling slightly. The creature, sensing her gentle nature, nuzzled against her palm, its touch sending a warm current through her body.

A wave of relief washed over Raju. Seeing the creature's peaceful demeanor melt away his initial apprehension. A grin, wide and genuine, spread across his face. This wasn't just an adventure; it was the beginning of something extraordinary.

THE CAVERN ECHOED WITH Kiran's gasp as the tiny creature, its iridescent wings shimmering, landed on her outstretched finger. A sense of wonderment, tinged with a touch of trepidation, filled her. This fantastical world, untouched by time, pulsed with an ancient energy that both terrified and exhilarated her.

Raju, ever the pragmatist, watched the exchange with a raised eyebrow. His hand instinctively reached for the slingshot tucked in his pocket, a reflex honed from years of childhood adventures navigating the wilds around their village. But as the creature nestled against Kiran's palm, its gentle demeanor dispelling any initial fear, a grin tugged at the corner of his lips. This wasn't just another escapade; it was the threshold to a world beyond imagination.

The creature, sensing their peaceful intentions, chirped melodically, the sound resonating deep within Kiran. An inexplicable certainty bloomed in her chest – this wasn't a mere creature, but a guide, a guardian of this hidden realm. With a tentative hand, her fingers trembling ever so slightly, she reached out and stroked its head. The creature, its large, intelligent eyes filled with an ancient wisdom, nuzzled closer, its touch sending a surge of warmth through her.

Suddenly, the cavern floor trembled, a low rumble emanating from the depths. The bioluminescent plants flickered momentarily, casting grotesque shadows on the cavern walls. Kiran and Raju exchanged a startled glance, their hearts pounding in unison. The playful wonder in the air was replaced by a chilling sense of foreboding.

The tiny creature on Kiran's finger trilled sharply, its wings buzzing frantically. It fluttered towards the silver tree at the center of the cavern, its soft glow intensifying as if beckoning them to follow. Without hesitation, Kiran and Raju followed the creature's lead, their initial awe morphing into a desperate urge to understand the sudden shift in the atmosphere.

As they approached the silver tree, its emerald leaves pulsed with an ever-brighter light. The creature landed on a branch, its chirps growing more frantic. Kiran felt a strange pull towards the tree, an invisible force urging her closer. Hesitantly, she reached out and placed her hand on the smooth bark.

A jolt of energy surged through her, coursing through her veins like a bolt of lightning. Images, vivid and fleeting, flooded her mind – a forgotten civilization, a race of beings attuned to nature's rhythm, a world ravaged by a force unseen. The visions came and went in a whirlwind, leaving behind a profound sense of loss and a burning question: what had happened to this once-thriving world?

As abruptly as they began, the visions ceased. Kiran stumbled back, overwhelmed by the sudden influx of emotions and knowledge. Raju, his face etched with concern, rushed to her side, his hand catching hers in a reassuring grip.

"Kiran, what happened?" he asked, his voice laced with worry.

Kiran shook her head, speechless. The visions, though fleeting, felt strangely real, a part of a forgotten past echoing in the caverns of her mind. Looking back at the silver tree, she noticed an inscription etched on its bark, glowing with an ethereal light. The symbols, similar to the ones adorning the hidden doorway, seemed to writhe and twist, beckoning her to decipher their meaning.

Driven by an inexplicable urge, Kiran reached out and touched the inscription. A surge of energy crackled between her fingertips and the inscription, and the symbols flared brightly. The cavern floor trembled once more, a deafening roar echoing through the vast space. The ground beneath their feet split open, revealing a hidden passage that plunged into darkness.

The tiny creature swooped down, landing on Kiran's shoulder and chirping insistently. It then darted towards the gaping passage, urging them to follow. Fear threatened to consume Kiran, but the creature's unwavering faith and the weight of the forgotten civilization she had glimpsed in the visions spurred her forward.

Taking a deep breath, she squeezed Raju's hand. "We have to go," she said, her voice surprisingly steady despite the tremor in her heart.

Raju, ever the loyal friend, nodded silently. He knew the look in her eyes – the unwavering determination that had always propelled them on their childhood adventures. Together, they stepped into the darkness, the bioluminescent creature leading the way, its tiny form a beacon in the inky blackness.

The passage was narrow and damp, the air thick with the smell of ancient stone and something metallic that sent shivers down their spines. The only sound was the rhythmic drip of water somewhere in the distance and the soft thud of their footsteps on the rough-hewn steps that led deeper into the earth.

As they descended, the passage twisted and turned, each bend revealing a deeper layer of this hidden world. The walls were adorned with faded murals depicting scenes from the lost civilization.

As they descended, the passage twisted and turned, each bend revealing a deeper layer of this hidden world. The walls were adorned with faded murals depicting scenes from the lost civilization – scenes of harmony with nature, intricate technological marvels, and a final battle against a shadowy, formless entity.

The murals fueled a fire of curiosity within Kiran. Who were these people? What was the nature of the enemy they faced? Had their civilization succumbed to this unseen force? The weight of these questions pressed heavily on her mind.

The passage finally opened into a vast cavern, far grander than the one they had left above. Here, the air shimmered with an otherworldly luminescence, emanating from a colossal crystal sphere suspended in the center. The sphere pulsed with a rhythmic energy, and within its depths, swirling mist formed fleeting images – images of a dying world choked by a thick, black fog.

As they approached the sphere, the tiny creature on Kiran's shoulder chirped urgently. It then darted towards the sphere, its iridescent wings catching the ethereal light. Kiran felt an undeniable pull towards the sphere, a magnetic force urging her closer. Hesitantly, she reached out and placed her hand on its smooth surface.

A wave of energy surged through her, more powerful than before. This time, the visions were clearer, more detailed. She saw the once-vibrant world slowly succumbing to a creeping darkness, a miasma that corrupted everything it touched. The beings of light fought valiantly, wielding the power of the crystal sphere, but their efforts seemed futile against the relentless tide of darkness.

The final vision struck Kiran with the force of a physical blow. She saw a lone figure, cloaked in light, channeling the sphere's energy into a final, desperate attack. The darkness recoiled, momentarily stunned, but it was not enough. The figure faltered, its light flickering before being extinguished by the encroaching shadows.

Kiran gasped, reeling back from the sphere. The weight of the vision settled upon her like a shroud. The lost civilization, their valiant struggle, their ultimate demise – it all felt terrifyingly real. Tears welled up in her eyes, a silent tribute to their sacrifice.

Suddenly, a soft, melodic voice echoed through the cavern, resonating within Kiran's mind. It was a voice filled with sorrow and a flicker of hope.

"The guardian has fallen," the voice spoke, "but the light remains. You, chosen one, hold the key to our redemption."

Kiran spun around, searching for the source of the voice, but the cavern remained empty. The only sound was the rhythmic hum of the crystal sphere and the frantic chirping of the creature on her shoulder.

"Who are you?" she whispered, her voice trembling slightly.

"We are the echoes of the past," the voice replied, "guiding you towards a chance to rewrite our fate."

The weight of the revelation settled upon Kiran's shoulders. Chosen one? How could a simple village girl be the key to saving a lost civilization? Doubt gnawed at her, but the memory of the final vision, the lone figure sacrificing everything for a sliver of hope, steeled her resolve.

Looking back at the crystal sphere, Kiran felt a surge of determination. She didn't fully understand what she had to do, but she knew she couldn't ignore the call. With newfound purpose, she turned to Raju, her eyes filled with a mixture of fear and determination.

"Raju," she said, her voice surprisingly steady, "we have a lot to learn."

Chapter 2: Echoes of the Past

The revelation in the cavern echoed in Kiran's mind like a haunting melody. Chosen one? The weight of the title felt both exhilarating and terrifying. How could a simple girl from a small village be the key to saving a lost civilization? Doubt gnawed at her, whispering insidious uncertainties. Yet, the memory of the final vision – the lone figure sacrificing everything for a sliver of hope – burned bright in her mind, fanning the embers of determination within her.

Gazing back at the colossal crystal sphere, its ethereal glow casting an otherworldly light on the cavern walls, Kiran felt a surge of purpose course through her. The path ahead remained shrouded in mystery, but the echoes of the past, their plea for redemption, resonated deeply within her.

Turning to Raju, her childhood companion and her constant source of strength, she met his gaze. A silent conversation passed between them, a shared flicker of apprehension laced with unwavering support. Raju, ever the pragmatist, had always grounded Kiran's flights of fancy. Now, however, his eyes held a newfound respect, a recognition of the extraordinary burden she carried.

"Raju," Kiran began, her voice surprisingly steady despite the tremor in her heart, "we have a lot to learn."

Raju offered a reassuring smile, the familiar warmth in his eyes a comforting constant amidst the swirling uncertainties. "Together," he replied, his voice firm.

With a silent nod, they emerged from the cavern, the tiny creature – their newfound guide – flitting ahead, its iridescent wings catching the faint luminescence filtering down from the world above. The once-awe-inspiring passage now seemed less daunting, a familiar path leading back to the fantastical world they had stumbled upon.

As they ascended, the bioluminescent plants cast an ethereal glow on their path, their soft luminescence painting the cavern walls in a kaleidoscope of colors. The silver tree at the cavern's heart shimmered with an otherworldly light, a beacon amidst the deepening shadows.

Reaching the hidden doorway, they emerged into the twilight embrace of the approaching dusk. The familiar scent of damp earth and decaying leaves, once comforting in its familiarity, now seemed tinged with a melancholic reminder of the world they were leaving behind.

The last rays of the setting sun cast long shadows across the ruins, painting the crumbling walls in hues of orange and gold. The air, once heavy with the oppressive silence of the forgotten fort, now hummed with the chirping of crickets and the rustling of leaves, a symphony of life that soothed the disquietude in their hearts.

As they stood at the threshold of their world, the weight of their newfound knowledge settled upon them. The fantastical world they had glimpsed wasn't just a figment of Kiran's imagination; it was a hidden reality teeming with its own history, its own struggles. The echoes of the past, their desperate plea for redemption, resonated in the quiet moments, urging them to act.

But where to begin? The vastness of the task before them felt overwhelming. Kiran, a dreamer by nature, often found solace in the fantastical worlds conjured by her imagination. Now, however, that very imagination felt burdened by the weight of reality.

Raju, ever the strategist, observed her silent contemplation. "We need a plan," he said, his voice breaking the comfortable silence.

Kiran glanced at him, a spark of gratitude igniting within her. "A plan," she echoed, the weight of the word settling on her shoulders.

They settled under the shade of a gnarled banyan tree, its ancient branches cradling them like a protective embrace. The chirping of crickets and the hooting of owls provided a gentle soundtrack to their brainstorming session.

"The voice in the cavern mentioned the crystal sphere," Kiran began, her voice barely a whisper. "Maybe that's the key. If we can understand its power, maybe we can find a way to help those beings of light."

Raju nodded thoughtfully. "But how do we even begin to understand something like that? It's unlike anything we've ever seen before."

Silence descended once more, broken only by the rustling of leaves in the night breeze. Kiran closed her eyes, willing herself to delve deeper into the memories of the visions. The final image, the lone figure channeling the sphere's energy, flickered before her mind's eye.

Suddenly, a memory from her childhood surfaced, a memory long forgotten but inexplicably vivid in that moment. Her grandfather, a wizened old man with eyes that held the wisdom of a thousand stories, used to speak of a hidden knowledge passed down through generations, a knowledge about harnessing the power of nature's elements.

A gasp escaped her lips. Could there be a connection? Could her grandfather's stories hold the key to unlocking the secrets

THE SUCCESS OF MANIPULATING the sun's energy fueled Kiran and Raju's determination. They practiced diligently, pushing the boundaries of their newfound abilities. Each day brought a new experiment, a new test of their connection with nature.

Kiran, with her innate affinity for the mystical, blossomed under the tutelage of the ancient scrolls. She learned to manipulate the flow of water, coaxing a neglected wellspring at the village's edge back to life. The once-parched land drank deeply, the earth responding with a vibrant burst of wildflowers that sprung up seemingly overnight. The villagers, initially skeptical of Kiran's newfound powers, watched in awe as the barren well overflowed with crystal-clear water.

Raju, ever the pragmatist, found his connection with nature less intuitive. Yet, with newfound respect for the natural world, he discovered a surprising knack for calming the wind. A potent storm, brewing on the horizon, threatened to unleash its fury upon their village. Guided by the cryptic symbols in the scrolls,

Raju focused his will, his voice harmonizing with the howling wind. Slowly, the storm abated, the churning clouds dispersing into a tapestry of tranquil blue. The villagers, who had braced themselves for the storm's onslaught, cheered in gratitude, hailing Raju as a savior.

As their connection with nature deepened, so did their understanding of the scrolls. They deciphered tales of the guardians of light, the beings who had once used the crystal sphere to maintain balance in their world. These guardians, attuned to the rhythm of nature, channeled the sphere's energy to nurture life and repel darkness.

But the scrolls also spoke of a chilling adversary – the Blight. A creeping entity fueled by negativity, the Blight devoured life force, leaving behind a wasteland of barren soil and withered flora. The visions from the cavern resurfaced in Kiran's mind – the once-vibrant world choked by the thick black fog, the valiant struggle of the guardians, their eventual demise.

A shiver ran down Kiran's spine. The Blight, it seemed, wasn't just a threat from a forgotten past; it was a living entity, its tendrils reaching towards their world. The weight of this knowledge settled upon them like a shroud. They weren't just learning to harness nature's power; they were preparing for a war against an unseen enemy.

One moonlit night, under the watchful gaze of a million stars, Kiran and Raju sat by the banyan tree, their usual meeting place. The silence was heavy with unspoken anxieties. Kiran broke the stillness, her voice barely a whisper.

"The Blight," she said, the word hanging heavy in the air. "It's coming, isn't it?"

Raju nodded, his face grim. "The scrolls talk about a distortion, a tear in the fabric separating our worlds. The Blight is using this tear to seep into our world."

"We need to find that tear," Kiran stated, her voice firm despite the tremor in her heart. "If we can seal it, maybe we can stop the Blight before it spreads."

Raju squeezed her hand reassuringly. "We'll find it, Kiran. Together."

Their journey to locate the tear became their singular focus. The ancient scrolls offered cryptic clues – faint tremors in the earth, a sudden shift in the wind patterns, a distortion in the night sky. Kiran and Raju, armed with their newfound abilities and a renewed sense of purpose, embarked on a quest that stretched far beyond the boundaries of their village.

Days bled into weeks as they traversed dense forests and vast plains, their senses attuned to the subtle whispers of nature. They faced challenges along the way – treacherous mountain passes, encounters with wild animals, and the ever-present fear of the Blight's touch. But their bond, forged in years of childhood adventures and strengthened by their shared responsibility, held them together.

One afternoon, as they journeyed through a desolate wasteland, they stumbled upon an anomaly. The once-fertile land lay barren, the air thick with a sense of oppressive silence. Even the insects, usually a vibrant part of the ecosystem, were absent. Kiran felt a prickling sensation on her skin, a cold touch that sent shivers down her spine.

"This is it," she whispered, her voice barely audible. "The Blight's touch."

Raju reached for her hand, his grip firm. "We're close, Kiran. I can feel it."

The tear, they realized, wouldn't be a physical object but a distortion in the natural order. Guided by the scrolls and their heightened senses, they spent days searching, their determination growing with each passing moment. Finally, on a hill overlooking the desolate wasteland, they found it – a swirling vortex in the air, a tear in the fabric separating their world

The swirling vortex in the air pulsed with an unnatural energy, a gaping maw in the fabric of reality. A stench of decay and corruption wafted from the tear, chilling Kiran and Raju to the bone. This, then, was the entry point for the Blight, the source of the creeping darkness that threatened their world.

A mixture of fear and determination coursed through Kiran. This was the culmination of their journey, the moment where everything they had learned would be put to the test. She glanced at Raju, his face etched with concern but unwavering resolve. Together, they had to find a way to seal the tear, to push back the encroaching darkness.

The scrolls, their only guide in this uncharted territory, offered a glimmer of hope. They spoke of a ritual, a complex dance with the elements, that could potentially bind the tear shut. But performing such a ritual would require immense power, a perfect harmony with nature that they hadn't fully mastered.

Doubt gnawed at Kiran's heart. Were they ready for such a task? Were they powerful enough to withstand the Blight's corrupting influence? But the desolate wasteland stretching before them, a testament to the Blight's destructive power, served as a stark reminder of the consequences of failure.

Taking a deep breath, Kiran turned to Raju. "We can do this," she said, her voice firm despite the tremor within. "We have to try."

Raju met her gaze, a silent understanding passing between them. He nodded, a flicker of determination replacing his initial apprehension. Together, they walked towards the swirling vortex, the air growing colder and thicker with each step.

The scrolls described the ritual in detail, a series of intricate movements and ancient chants that resonated with the elements. Kiran stood facing the vortex, its malevolent energy pressing against her like a physical barrier. She closed her eyes, focusing on the information gleaned from the scrolls. With each breath, she visualized the power of the sun, its life-giving energy a counterpoint to the Blight's darkness.

Raju, positioned behind her, channeled the calming flow of water, his voice weaving a melody that countered the Blight's corrupting whispers. As they chanted, the air crackled with unseen energy. Kiran felt a surge of power within her, the warmth of the sun coursing through her veins. The vortex writhed in response, its unnatural energy battling against the forces they commanded.

The ritual reached its climax. Kiran, with a burst of concentrated energy, channeled the power of the sun towards the vortex. A blinding flash erupted, pushing back the darkness momentarily. In that split second, Raju seized the opportunity. With a final, powerful surge of his water-based energy, he wove a binding spell around the vortex's edges.

Silence descended, thick and heavy. The vortex pulsed weakly, its power significantly diminished. Kiran and Raju, drained but exhilarated, watched as the unnatural light slowly faded, the tear in reality slowly mending itself.

A joyous whoop escaped Raju's lips. They had done it! They had sealed the tear, pushing back the Blight's immediate threat. Relief washed over Kiran, her knees buckling beneath the weight of the ordeal. They had faced the darkness and emerged victorious, their bond strengthened by their shared courage.

However, as they caught their breath, a flicker of concern shadowed Kiran's joy. The Blight itself remained, a festering wound in another world. The scrolls spoke of a final battle, a confrontation with the source of the darkness itself. Sealing the tear had merely bought them time, a chance to prepare for the inevitable conflict.

As the sun peeked over the horizon, casting its golden light on the scarred land, Kiran and Raju knew their journey was far from over. They had taken a significant step, but the true test of their courage, their connection with nature, and their bond as friends, still lay ahead. The battle for their world had just begun. The echoes of the past, the pleas of a lost civilization, now resonated within them, a call to arms that they couldn't ignore. With newfound resolve, they turned back towards their village, their hearts heavy with the weight of responsibility, but their spirits buoyed by the knowledge that they were not alone in this fight. They had each other, and the spirit of nature as their guide.

The arduous journey back to their village was shrouded in a newfound urgency. The success of sealing the tear offered a flicker of hope, but the knowledge of the Blight's true nature cast a long shadow. Kiran and Raju carried the weight of their responsibility heavily, their quiet camaraderie a source of strength in the face of the looming darkness.

News of their exploits, traveling faster than their own pace, had preceded them. Upon reaching the village, they were met with a mix of awe and trepidation. Kiran, once a dreamer relegated to fantastical stories, was now hailed as a savior, the one who had quelled the storm and brought life back to the barren well. Raju, ever the pragmatist, found himself thrust into the role of protector, a shield against the unseen threats that lurked beyond the veil of reality.

The villagers, initially wary of their newfound abilities, gradually warmed to the idea of protectors attuned to the whispers of nature. Kiran, with her gentle touch and blossoming connection to the elements, became a beacon of hope, inspiring others to see the world around them with fresh eyes. Raju, with his calming presence and practical know-how, emerged as a leader, devising strategies to prepare the village for the unknown.

Days turned into weeks, then months, as Kiran and Raju diligently honed their abilities. The ancient scrolls, their cryptic language now a familiar melody, became their constant companions. They practiced channeling the power of the elements, not just for defense but also to nurture and heal. Kiran, under the watchful gaze of the banyan tree, learned to coax barren land back to life, her touch fostering the growth of vibrant flora. Raju, spending hours by the village well, mastered the art of manipulating water, ensuring a bountiful supply for the entire community.

Their newfound roles, however, came with a heavy burden. The whispers of the Blight, a constant thrumming at the back of their minds, served as a chilling reminder of the impending battle. Kiran, tormented by nightmares of the Blight's corrupting influence, sought solace in the whispers of the wind, the rustling leaves offering a calming melody. Raju, haunted by visions of desolation, found solace in the gurgling water of the well, its steady flow a soothing counterpoint to the Blight's malevolent energy.

One starlit night, as they sat by their usual spot under the banyan tree, Kiran broke the silence. "The scrolls," she began, her voice tinged with worry, "they speak of a weapon, a key to defeating the Blight."

Raju nodded, his brow furrowed in concentration. "There are fragmented references, but nothing concrete. It seems like knowledge lost to time."

A wave of frustration washed over Kiran. They had come so far, yet the answer to ultimate victory remained elusive. But she refused to give in to despair. The villagers, who trusted them with their lives, deserved a chance.

"We can't give up," she stated, her voice firm despite the tremor in her heart. "There has to be something in the scrolls, some clue we haven't noticed yet."

Raju squeezed her hand, his eyes reflecting a quiet determination. "We'll find it, Kiran. Together."

Their search for the weapon intensified. They spent countless hours poring over the scrolls, deciphering cryptic symbols, searching for hidden meanings. They consulted with the village elders, hoping to glean any wisdom passed down through generations. Even the villagers themselves were enlisted in the search, their keen eyes scanning ancient murals and forgotten ruins for any hint that might lead them to the key.

Days bled into weeks, but their efforts met with a frustrating silence. Doubt began to creep in, gnawing at their resolve. Was the weapon a mere myth, a figment of the past? Had they misread the scrolls, misinterpreted the guardians' messages?

Just as despair threatened to engulf them, a breakthrough arrived in an unexpected form. An old shepherd, known for his uncanny ability to understand the language of birds, approached Kiran and Raju with a startling revelation. He spoke of a hidden cave, deep within the mountains, where an ancient bird, rumored to be the guardian of forgotten knowledge, resided. The bird, according to the legends, might hold the key to unlocking the weapon against the Blight.

A flicker of hope ignited within them. This was the lead they had been desperately seeking, a chance to find the weapon and face the Blight on equal footing. With renewed purpose, Kiran and Raju embarked on a new journey, one that led them deep into the heart of the mountains, towards a confrontation with the legendary bird and the secrets it held.

Chapter 3: Whispers on the Wind

The journey to the mountains was fraught with challenges. The path, seldom traveled and overgrown with dense vegetation, tested their endurance. Towering cliffs cast long shadows, and the air grew thin and crisp with each step upwards. But Kiran and Raju pressed on, fueled by a renewed sense of purpose. The shepherd's tale of the ancient bird, a potential holder of the key to defeating the Blight, resonated deeply within them.

Days bled into weeks as they navigated treacherous slopes, crossed gushing rivers, and traversed through dense, ancient forests teeming with unseen eyes. They relied on their newfound connection with nature to guide them. Kiran, attuned to the whispers of the wind, identified safe passage through treacherous gusts. Raju, sensitive to the earth's tremors, steered them clear of potential landslides.

Their bond, forged in the crucible of their trials, had grown stronger than ever. Kiran's impulsive nature was tempered by Raju's pragmatism, while Raju's anxieties were soothed by Kiran's unwavering optimism. They learned to trust each other implicitly, their communication a seamless language of shared glances and unspoken understanding.

One moonlit night, as they camped by a crystal-clear stream, a sense of foreboding descended upon them. The air grew heavy with an unnatural stillness, and a chilling silence blanketed the forest. The nocturnal creatures, once chirping their lullabies, fell eerily quiet. Even the leaves on the trees seemed to hold their breath.

Raju, his hand instinctively reaching for the hilt of his makeshift dagger fashioned from a sharpened branch, spoke in a hushed tone. "There's something wrong here, Kiran. I can feel it."

Kiran nodded, a shiver running down her spine. The whispers of the wind, once playful and reassuring, now carried a faint echo of malice. It was a feeling she had grown all too familiar with – the corrupting touch of the Blight.

Suddenly, a guttural growl ripped through the silence, making the very ground tremble beneath their feet. Before they could react, shadowy figures emerged from the darkness. Their hulking forms, grotesque parodies of wolves, bore the telltale signs of the Blight's touch – twisted limbs, glowing red eyes, and a stench of decay that hung heavy in the air.

Kiran and Raju exchanged a determined look. They had come too far to turn back now. With a synchronized yell, they channeled their connection with nature. Kiran, with a gesture of her hand, summoned a swirling vortex of wind that buffeted the creatures, momentarily disrupting their attack. Raju, his voice a soothing chant, manipulated the water from the nearby stream, creating a slick path that sent the creatures tumbling on their misshapen bodies.

The battle was fierce, a testament to the Blight's corrupting influence. The creatures, driven by a primal hunger, were relentless. Kiran conjured gusts of wind that sent them flying, while Raju manipulated the water to trip and disorient them. Yet, with each attack, the creatures rose again, their twisted forms fueled by the Blight's dark energy.

Just as exhaustion began to set in, Kiran spotted a jagged crack in the mountain face behind the creatures. Focusing her remaining energy, she channeled a powerful blast of wind, creating a miniature whirlwind. The wind tore through the crack, dislodging a massive boulder that tumbled down the mountainside with a thunderous roar.

The boulder struck the Blight-corrupted wolves with an earth-shaking impact, burying them under a cascade of rock and debris. Kiran and Raju collapsed onto the ground, gasping for breath. Their victory was short-lived, but it had bought them some much-needed rest and a renewed sense of urgency. They had faced the Blight's minions directly and emerged victorious, albeit barely.

The encounter served as a stark reminder of the growing threat. The Blight, it seemed, wasn't content with waiting for the tear to heal. It was actively sending its corrupted agents to hinder their search for the weapon. They couldn't afford to waste any more time. The mountains loomed before them, their peaks shrouded in an ethereal mist. Somewhere within, the ancient bird awaited, and with it, perhaps the key to saving their world.

As the first rays of dawn painted the sky with streaks of gold, Kiran and Raju rose, their bodies aching but their spirits unbroken. Filled with a renewed sense of purpose, they pressed on towards the mountains, their hearts pounding with anticipation and the echoes of the wind whispering secrets of what lay ahead.

The arduous climb through the mountains pushed Kiran and Raju to their physical and mental limits. The thin air bit at their lungs, and the relentless incline made their legs scream in protest. But the memory of the Blight-corrupted wolves spurred them forward. They couldn't afford to falter, not when the fate of their world rested on their shoulders.

Days bled into one another, marked by the relentless climb and the breathtaking vistas that unfolded before them. Lush valleys cradled by snow-capped peaks gave way to barren plateaus scoured by wind and time. Kiran, with her heightened connection to nature, felt a deep reverence for the raw beauty surrounding them. The whispering wind carried stories of ancient glaciers and the resilience of life clinging to the harshest environments.

One evening, as they huddled around a crackling fire, Raju pointed towards a distant peak, its summit shrouded in a perpetual mist. "The shepherd mentioned that the bird's cave lies somewhere on the slopes of that mountain," he said, his voice raspy from the dry air.

Kiran stared at the peak, a sense of foreboding washing over her. The swirling mist seemed to hold an unnerving presence, a barrier protecting whatever secrets lay within. "Do you think it's safe?" she asked, a tremor in her voice.

Raju, ever the pragmatist, shrugged. "There's only one way to find out," he replied, his gaze unwavering.

The next morning, they embarked on the final leg of their journey. The air grew colder, the wind whistling a mournful tune. The path narrowed, becoming a treacherous scramble over loose rocks and treacherous ledges. The swirling mist grew denser, obscuring the way and making navigation a perilous task.

Suddenly, the ground beneath Kiran's feet gave way. With a scream, she tumbled down a steep incline, tumbling through the swirling mist until she landed with a painful thud on a rocky surface. Disoriented and bruised, she struggled to her feet, her vision blurry and her ears ringing.

"Raju!" she cried out, her voice swallowed by the thick mist. Panic clawed at her throat as silence descended, broken only by the howling wind. Had she fallen too far? Was she alone? Just as despair threatened to consume her, a soft cooing sound echoed through the mist.

Curious, Kiran followed the sound, her hand instinctively outstretched for support. The ground beneath her leveled out, and the mist seemed to thin slightly. Squinting through the haze, she saw a majestic bird perched on a rocky outcrop. Its feathers shimmered with a spectrum of colors that seemed to shift and change in the dim light.

The bird's eyes, intelligent and ancient, locked onto Kiran's. As their eyes met, Kiran felt a wave of calmness wash over her. Fear and panic receded, replaced by a sense of awe and reverence. This, without a doubt, was the guardian of the cave.

"Greetings, young one," a voice resonated in Kiran's mind, not spoken but somehow understood. "You have come seeking knowledge."

Kiran could not reply, overwhelmed by the sheer presence of the bird. But the guardian understood. In a series of mental images, Kiran experienced the bird's memories – the rise and fall of civilizations, the encroaching darkness of the Blight, and the guardians' desperate struggle.

Finally, the vision shifted. Kiran saw a weapon, a magnificent sword forged from starlight and imbued with the power of nature. It was a weapon unlike any she had ever seen, capable of channeling the very essence of life itself.

"The key to defeating the Blight," the bird's voice resonated again. "But the power it wields comes at a great cost. Are you prepared to bear the burden?"

Kiran looked at the magnificent weapon, an image burned into her mind. She knew the answer. The fate of her world rested on her shoulders. "Yes," she answered, her voice firm despite the tremor within her.

Kiran's voice echoed through the swirling mist, a beacon of unwavering resolve. The ancient bird, its gaze penetrating her very soul, studied her for a long, silent moment. Finally, it spoke, its voice resonating within Kiran's mind.

"The weapon is yours," it intoned, the air crackling with an unseen energy. "But remember, young one, it is not a mere tool. It is an extension of your own will, your connection to nature. Wield it with respect, for its power can be both a shield and a scourge."

A shimmering light erupted from the bird's outstretched wing, revealing the very weapon Kiran had witnessed in the vision. The sword, forged from starlight, pulsed with an ethereal energy that sent shivers down her spine. Its hilt, carved from an unknown wood that seemed to breathe with the rhythm of nature, felt warm and welcoming in her grasp.

As Kiran held the sword aloft, the mist around them swirled and dissipated, revealing the entrance to a hidden cave. The air emanating from the cave mouth hummed with a potent energy, a testament to the knowledge and power held within.

"The secrets you seek lie within," the bird said, its voice softer now, tinged with a hint of melancholy. "But remember, the path will be fraught with challenges. You must face your deepest fears and unlock your true potential if you are to wield the weapon and defend your world."

With a final piercing cry, the bird spread its magnificent wings and soared into the swirling mist, disappearing from sight. Kiran stood there, the weight of the sword and the bird's words heavy on her heart. She looked at Raju, who had just emerged from the mist, a worried expression etched on his face.

"I found it, Raju," she said, her voice filled with awe and a touch of fear. "The weapon."

Raju's eyes widened as he saw the sword, its ethereal glow illuminating their surroundings. Relief and concern battled within him. "Thank goodness," he breathed, his voice hoarse. "But are you sure you can handle it?"

Kiran met his gaze, a newfound determination gleaming in her eyes. "I don't have a choice," she said resolutely. "The Blight grows stronger every day. We must return and prepare for the battle that awaits us."

The journey back down the mountain was fraught with challenges. The descent was treacherous, and the encounter with the Blight-corrupted wolves had taken its toll. But Kiran, fueled by a newfound purpose, pushed forward. The weight of the weapon on her back was a constant reminder of the responsibility she now bore.

Back in the village, their return was met with a mix of joy and apprehension. Whispers of their encounter with the Blight and the legendary bird spread like wildfire. Kiran and Raju, once considered mere storytellers, were now hailed as heroes destined to lead them into battle.

The following weeks were a whirlwind of activity. Kiran spent countless hours training with the weapon, learning to channel its power through meditation and practice. The sword, once a vision, became an extension of herself. Raju, with his newfound understanding of the villagers' anxieties, focused on bolstering their defenses and preparing them for the potential Blight incursion.

Days turned into weeks, then months. The villagers, inspired by Kiran and Raju's dedication, worked tirelessly to fortify the village. Watchtowers were erected, lookout points established, and every able-bodied villager learned basic self-defense. Despite the looming threat, a spirit of unity and resilience blossomed within the community.

One evening, as Kiran sat on the familiar spot under the banyan tree, the unmistakable tendrils of the Blight materialized on the horizon. A thick, black fog rolled in, choking the air and casting an oppressive silence over the village. The long-dreaded war had finally begun.

Kiran rose, the sword in her hand humming with power. Her gaze met Raju's, a silent communication passing between them. They were ready. The whispers of the wind carried the villagers' cheers and prayers, a wave of support that surged through Kiran. This wasn't just her battle; it was a fight for the very fabric of their existence.

With a battle cry that echoed through the valley, Kiran charged towards the encroaching darkness, the weight of the sword and the fate of her world resting on her shoulders. The battle for their world had begun, and Kiran, the girl who once dreamt of fantastical creatures, now stood at the forefront, a warrior wielding the power of nature itself.

The Blight rolled in like a tide of suffocating darkness. The once-vibrant horizon was swallowed by a thick, oily fog that choked the air and cast an unnatural stillness over the village. Kiran, the weight of the starlit sword heavy on her back, felt a tremor course through her body - a mixture of fear and determination. Glancing at Raju, she saw a mirror of her own emotions reflected in his steely gaze.

The villagers, no longer mere bystanders, stood shoulder to shoulder, armed with makeshift weapons and a fierce determination to protect their homes. Their cheers, though tinged with anxiety, provided Kiran with a surge of courage. With a deep breath, she raised the sword high, its ethereal glow cutting through the encroaching darkness like a beacon of hope.

The Blight responded with a chorus of guttural growls. From the swirling fog emerged twisted creatures, parodies of life warped by the Blight's corrupting touch. They were a grotesque amalgamation of monstrous shapes, all driven by a single purpose - to consume and destroy.

The battle commenced with a ferocious clash. Kiran, guided by her enhanced connection to nature, weaved through the battlefield with an almost otherworldly grace. The starlit sword, humming with celestial power, met the crude weapons of the Blight creatures with devastating results. With each swipe, Kiran channeled the life force of the earth, her movements imbued with a power that seemed to disintegrate the Blight's creations on contact.

Raju, ever the strategist, used his mastery over water to disrupt the Blight's movements. He created slick pathways, hindering their advance and sending them crashing into each other in a chaotic mess. The villagers, inspired by their leaders, fought with newfound bravery. They used whatever they could – pitchforks, torches, and even their bare hands - to push back the tide of darkness.

The battle raged on, a cacophony of clashing weapons, guttural roars, and cries of pain. Kiran, fueled by the villagers' desperate pleas and the sword's potent energy, fought with unwavering determination. Yet, with each Blight creature vanquished, two more seemed to rise from the swirling fog, a seemingly endless horde fueled by the darkness itself.

Just as exhaustion began to overwhelm them, a wave of despair threatening to engulf their hearts, a horrifying creature emerged from the Blight. This monstrosity, far larger than anything they had encountered before, resembled a grotesque combination of all the creatures they had fought. Its eyes, burning embers of pure malice, focused on Kiran, recognizing her as the greatest threat.

A primal fear threatened to consume Kiran. The sheer power emanating from the creature was enough to make her knees buckle. But the thought of the villagers, their terrified faces etched in her mind, spurred her forward. She couldn't give in. Not now.

With a battle cry that echoed through the battlefield, Kiran channeled all her remaining energy into the starlit sword. The blade pulsed with an intense white light, almost blinding in its radiance. With a final, desperate swing, she lunged towards the Blight monstrosity, the fate of her world hanging in the balance.

Chapter 4: The Price of Starlight

The blinding white light from Kiran's starlit sword momentarily overwhelmed the battlefield. Villagers shielded their eyes, Blight creatures recoiled in fear, and even the monstrous entity flinched from the unexpected burst of power. In that split second, the air crackled with an intense energy that seemed to vibrate through the very fabric of reality.

When the light subsided, a heavy silence descended. Kiran, her body trembling from the exertion, lowered the sword. Her gaze darted around the battlefield, searching for any sign of movement. The Blight creatures, those that remained, lay scattered on the ground, lifeless husks of their former selves. The monstrous entity, its form flickering and unstable, had vanished without a trace.

A wave of relief washed over Kiran, so intense it almost made her legs give way. They had done it. Against all odds, they had repelled the Blight's initial attack. Cheers erupted from the villagers, a cacophony of joy and disbelief mixing with the groans of the wounded.

But amidst the celebration, a chilling realization dawned on Kiran. The sword, once humming with celestial power, felt heavy and strangely inert in her grasp. The vibrant glow that had illuminated the battlefield was replaced by a faint, flickering ember. A pang of fear shot through her heart.

Raju, sensing her distress, rushed to her side. "Kiran, are you alright?" he asked, his voice laced with concern.

Kiran managed a weak smile, her gaze fixed on the sword. "I'm fine," she said, her voice barely a whisper. "But the sword..."

Raju followed her gaze, his face mirroring her apprehension. The bird's words echoed in their minds: "The power it wields comes at a great cost." Had Kiran paid that cost already? Was the sword a one-time weapon, its power expended in that single, desperate attack?

The cheers of the villagers died down, replaced by a nervous murmur. The Blight, though temporarily repelled, still loomed on the other side of the tear. Without the sword's power, how would they face a future attack? Despair threatened to consume them, but Kiran steeled her resolve.

"We may not have the sword at full power," she declared, her voice ringing with newfound determination, "but we still have each other. We have our connection to nature, and we have the courage to fight for our home."

Her words, imbued with a quiet strength, resonated with the villagers. They may have lost the sword's dazzling display of power, but they hadn't lost their spirit. The battle had revealed their resilience, their willingness to stand united against a seemingly insurmountable threat.

Days turned into weeks as the villagers, with renewed determination, focused on rebuilding their defenses and preparing for the inevitable second wave. Kiran, though worried about the sword's diminished power, devoted herself to training the villagers in basic combat techniques. She shared her understanding of nature, helping them tap into their own latent abilities to manipulate the elements.

Meanwhile, Raju, ever the strategist, analyzed the Blight's attack patterns, searching for weaknesses in their seemingly endless horde. He devised new defensive strategies, incorporating the villagers' newfound connection to nature into their tactics.

One starlit night, as Kiran sat under the banyan tree, the whispers on the wind carried a different message. It was faint, almost imperceptible, but there was a tremor of hope within it. The whispers spoke of a hidden wellspring, deep within the village forest, rumored to possess the power to heal and revitalize.

Hope surged through Kiran. Could this be the answer to restoring the sword's power? With a newfound determination, she embarked on a new quest, venturing deep into the forest, guided by the whispers of the wind and the faint tremor of hope within them.

The forest floor beneath Kiran's feet was a tapestry of fallen leaves, damp and cool against her bare toes. The air hung heavy with the scent of pine and decaying vegetation, a symphony of chirping crickets and rustling leaves providing the only music. Unlike the Blight's chilling fog, the forest pulsed with a quiet life force, a reassuring counterpoint to the darkness that threatened their world.

Kiran, guided by the ever-present whisper in the wind, moved deeper into the woods. The ancient trees, their branches gnarled and reaching, formed a natural canopy overhead, filtering the moonlight into a dappled pattern on the forest floor. She had ventured into these woods countless times as a child, exploring hidden streams and befriending the shy woodland creatures. Now, however, the familiar landscape held a sense of mystery, a feeling that secrets were waiting to be unearthed.

The whispers on the wind intensified, pulling her towards a clearing bathed in an ethereal glow. In the center stood a magnificent oak, its expansive branches forming a natural canopy cradling a shimmering pool of water. The water itself seemed to glow with an internal light, a mesmerizing blue that pulsed faintly in the darkness.

This was it. The wellspring. Kiran felt a surge of excitement tempered with caution. The wellspring's power resonated through her, a potent energy that whispered promises of rejuvenation and healing. But with such power came the possibility of danger. What were the consequences of harnessing its essence?

Hesitantly, Kiran approached the wellspring. As she neared, the water seemed to swirl and shift, reflecting the image of a woman with flowing white hair and eyes that shimmered like the moonlight itself. The woman smiled, a gentle warmth radiating from her presence.

"Welcome, child," the woman's voice echoed in Kiran's mind, a soft melody that soothed her anxieties. "You seek to restore what has been lost."

Kiran nodded, her voice catching in her throat. "The sword," she managed to whisper. "The Blight's attack drained its power. Do you have the means to revive it?"

The woman's smile softened. "The wellspring itself does not possess the power to directly restore the sword. However, it can provide you with what you need to reclaim its true potential."

She gestured towards the water. "Within this wellspring lies the essence of life, the very spark that animates the world. But remember, child, this power comes at a cost. You must be willing to offer something of equal value in return."

Kiran understood. The wellspring's essence wouldn't come freely. She had to give something up, something precious. But what did she have that equaled the sword's power? Her mind raced, searching for an answer, the fate of her world hanging in the balance.

Suddenly, a memory surfaced. A childhood incident, a foolish mistake for which she had never truly forgiven herself. She had accidentally injured a young deer while playing with a slingshot. The remorse she felt then, the guilt that had lingered all these years, washed over her.

Could this be the price? Could her own guilt, a burden she had carried for so long, be enough? It was a painful proposition, but the thought of facing the Blight without the sword's power was even more unbearable.

With tearful eyes, Kiran offered her sacrifice. "I am willing," she declared, her voice resolute. "Take my guilt, my regret. Let it be the price for restoring the sword's power."

As if in response, a tendril of ethereal light emerged from the wellspring, wrapping around Kiran. It surged through her, a cleansing wave that washed away years of self-recrimination. The pain of her past remained, a faint echo, but the suffocating weight of guilt had vanished.

The water in the wellspring shimmered, swirling more intensely than before. Kiran watched, mesmerized, as a vial filled with the same pulsating blue light materialized beside the pool. This, she understood, was the essence she needed.

With a final, gentle smile, the woman faded away, leaving Kiran alone with the vial and a newfound sense of peace. The forest floor no longer seemed shrouded in shadows, but bathed in an ethereal glow, a reflection of the wellspring's power coursing through her veins.

Holding the vial aloft, Kiran retraced her steps back towards the village. The whispering wind carried a renewed sense of hope, a melody that spoke of resilience and the strength within. The sword may be weakened, but she, Kiran, was no longer the same girl. The encounter at the wellspring had forged her anew, leaving behind the guilt and empowering her with a newfound resolve.

Back in the village, the atmosphere was tense. The initial euphoria of repelling the Blight had been replaced by a quiet anxiety. Without the sword's full power, they were all too

aware of their vulnerability. Kiran's arrival, the vial clutched tightly in her hand, brought a wave of both relief and curiosity.

Raju, who had been overseeing the training exercises, rushed to her side. "Kiran, you're back! Did you find it?" he asked, his voice laced with urgency.

Kiran nodded, a determined glint in her eyes. "The wellspring," she said, her voice hoarse from her journey. "It holds the essence of life, the power to revitalize."

The villagers gathered around, their faces etched with concern. Kiran explained her encounter with the woman at the wellspring, the price she had paid, and the vial filled with the pulsating blue light. A murmur of awe rippled through the crowd.

Elder Kaia, the village's most respected elder, stepped forward. Her weathered face, etched with the wisdom of years, held a glimmer of hope. "The legends speak of such a wellspring," she said, her voice raspy. "It is said to possess the power to heal not just the body, but the spirit as well."

Kiran looked at the vial, feeling a surge of responsibility. This wasn't just about restoring the sword's power; it was about using the wellspring's essence to strengthen the entire village, to prepare them for the inevitable final battle.

"We can't use it all on the sword," she declared, her voice ringing with conviction. "We need to share its power. We need everyone to be at their strongest to face the Blight."

A wave of agreement rippled through the crowd. Raju, ever the pragmatist, suggested a plan. They would divide the essence, using a small portion to revitalize the sword and the remaining majority to enhance the villagers' connection to nature.

The next few days were a blur of activity. Kiran, guided by Elder Kaia's knowledge of ancient rituals, carefully conducted the process of infusing the sword with the wellspring's essence. As she poured a single drop of the pulsating blue liquid onto the blade, a soft hum resonated through the air. The sword, once inert, pulsed with a renewed energy, the faint ember rekindled into a vibrant glow.

However, the transformation wasn't just visual. Kiran could feel a difference in the way the sword responded to her touch. It felt lighter, more responsive, as if it yearned to be wielded once more. But the true test of its power would come on the battlefield.

Meanwhile, the villagers underwent a transformation of their own. As they ingested small portions of the wellspring's essence, they felt a surge of energy coursing through their veins. Their connection to nature deepened, allowing them to manipulate the elements with greater control and precision.

Leaves danced around them at their command, water droplets coalesced into shields, and the wind obeyed their silent whispers.

The transformation wasn't uniform. Some villagers, like the young hunter Rohan, displayed a newfound control over fire. Others, like the wizened farmer Amara, could coax life back into barren soil with a mere touch. The wellspring's essence amplified their natural talents, turning them into a formidable force, a living network of nature's defenders.

Days turned into weeks, and the once-sleepy village buzzed with a newfound energy. Training exercises became more intense, fueled by the villagers' newfound connection to nature and their unwavering determination. Kiran, no longer just a dreamer but a leader, spearheaded their training, her own connection to the elements honed to a razor's edge. She could sense the Blight stirring on the other side of the tear, a malevolent presence growing stronger with each passing day.

One evening, as the villagers gathered around a crackling bonfire, a lookout stationed on the highest watchtower blew the signal horn, a long, mournful sound that echoed through the valley. The Blight was upon them.

Unlike the initial attack, this time the Blight came in waves. Grotesque creatures, twisted parodies of animals, surged forth from the swirling fog, their eyes burning with a malevolent hunger. But the villagers were ready.

Kiran, wielding the revitalized sword, led the charge. The blade, humming with celestial power, cleaved through the Blight creatures with ease. But the sheer number of them was overwhelming. As each creature fell, two more seemed to take its place.

Raju, at the center of the village, coordinated the defense. Villagers like Rohan unleashed a torrent of flames, driving back the Blight with a fiery wall. Amara, her touch imbued with the wellspring's essence, coaxed dormant vines to life, ensnaring and crushing the Blight creatures in their thick grasp.

The battle raged throughout the night, a cacophony of clashing weapons, guttural roars, and cries of defiance. Kiran fought with a ferocity born of desperation,

...her movements blurring as she channeled the wind into a whirlwind of razor-sharp blades, decimating the Blight creatures in her path. But exhaustion gnawed at her, a cold hand gripping her heart. The sword, though revitalized, remained a double-edged weapon. With every swing, a sliver of her own energy drained into the blade, fueling its power.

Yet, she couldn't falter. The villagers, emboldened by their early successes, were starting to show signs of fatigue. The Blight, relentless and driven by a dark purpose, pressed on, their monstrous forms crowding the village square.

Suddenly, a chilling shriek cut through the night. A monstrous figure, far larger and more grotesque than anything they had encountered before, emerged from the swirling fog. It resembled a skeletal dragon, its gaping maw lined with rows of jagged teeth, its eyes burning with an unholy light. This was the Blight's general, a harbinger of destruction.

A wave of despair threatened to engulf the villagers. But before Kiran could react, a blinding light erupted from the center of the village. The wellspring, seemingly untouched by the chaos, pulsed with a radiant blue light that surged outwards, enveloping the entire village in an ethereal shield.

The Blight creatures recoiled, screeching in pain as the light washed over them. Even the monstrous general recoiled, its eyes flickering with a flicker of fear. This wasn't part of the plan. The Blight, it seemed, wasn't prepared for the combined power of nature harnessed by the villagers.

The tide began to turn. The villagers, revitalized by the wellspring's shield and fueled by a renewed sense of hope, fought with a newfound ferocity. Rohan, his eyes blazing red, unleashed a torrent of fire that temporarily blinded the Blight general. Amara, her movements swift and sure, wove a web of vines that ensnared a group of Blight creatures, immobilizing them for the villagers to dispatch.

Kiran, seizing the opportunity, charged towards the Blight general. The sword hummed in her hand, a beacon of hope in the darkness. As they clashed, the ground trembled from the force of their blows. The Blight general, wielding a massive twisted blade, rained down blows fueled by malice. Kiran, drawing strength from the wind and the whispers of the wellspring's essence, parried and counterattacked, her movements a blur of grace and power.

The fight seemed to go on forever, a dance between life and death. Kiran felt her energy reserves dwindling with each blow, the sword demanding a heavy price for its devastating power. Yet, she couldn't give up. The fate of her world hung in the balance.

Just as exhaustion threatened to overwhelm her, she spotted an opening. With a final surge of strength, she channeled the wind through the blade, imbuing it with the power of a hurricane. The strike was true, the starlit sword cleaving through the Blight general's bony chest with a blinding flash of light.

The monstrous creature roared in agony, its form dissolving into a cloud of black smoke that dissipated in the night sky. As the smoke cleared, a stunned silence descended upon the battlefield. The Blight creatures, leaderless and demoralized, faltered for a moment.

Seeing this hesitation, the villagers let out a deafening roar that echoed through the valley. It was a primal cry of triumph, a testament to their resilience and their unwavering connection to nature. Taking advantage of the Blight's disarray, the villagers pressed their attack, driving the remaining creatures back into the swirling fog.

As the last tendrils of fog dissipated, revealing a clear, starlit sky, the villagers erupted in cheers. They had won. Exhausted but exhilarated, they embraced each other, their victory a testament to their unity and their newfound power.

Kiran, drained but triumphant, stood amidst the battlefield. The sword, its energy spent, lay heavy in her hand. Looking out at the village bathed in the pale moonlight, she knew this was just the beginning. The Blight, though crippled, wasn't destroyed. The tear still hung like a scar across the sky, a constant reminder of the threat that lurked beyond.

But for now, they had bought themselves time. Time to heal, to train, and to prepare for the next inevitable attack. As Kiran surveyed the faces around her, no longer filled with fear but with a newfound resolve, she knew they were ready. They were the guardians of their world, the children of nature, and they would not let the Blight consume all that they held dear. The battle for their world had begun, and though the future remained uncertain, Kiran, the girl who once dreamt of fantastical creatures, now stood as a symbol of hope, her heart filled with the whispers of the wind and the unwavering spirit of a true warrior.

Chapter 5: Whispers on the Wind

Weeks bled into months as the village settled into an uneasy peace. The scars of the Blight's attack remained – scorched earth where Rohan's flames had danced, patches of barren ground revitalized by Amara's touch, and a deep, hollow silence where the laughter of those lost in the battle once echoed. Yet, amidst the grief, a newfound resolve simmered within the hearts of the villagers.

Kiran, no longer just a village girl but a beacon of hope, shouldered the mantle of leadership with quiet strength. The villagers looked to her, their savior who wielded the starlit sword – a constant reminder of their victory and the ever-present threat.

The sword itself hung heavy on the wall in the village hall, a silent sentinel. Kiran had learned a harsh lesson during the battle. The sword's power, though immense, came at a terrible cost. Each swing drained a sliver of her own energy, leaving her feeling hollowed out. It was a weapon to be wielded with caution, a last resort in the fight for their survival.

Training continued, a constant hum of activity replacing the peaceful quietude of the past. The villagers, under Kiran's tutelage and Raju's strategic mind, honed their newfound connection to nature. They practiced channeling the wind's fury, coaxing life back into barren soil, and manipulating water into shields and weapons. The whispers of the forest, once a comforting background melody, became a source of guidance and power.

Kiran, too, delved deeper into her connection. Long hours were spent meditating under the banyan tree, seeking to understand the true essence of the starlit sword. The whispers on the wind, once faint and elusive, grew clearer, carrying fragments of forgotten lore and ancient knowledge.

One starlit night, as Kiran sat wrapped in meditation, a new message emerged from the whispers. It spoke of a hidden grove, nestled deep within the Whispering Woods, said to be a repository of forgotten knowledge – a place where the secrets of the starlit sword might be unlocked.

A spark of hope ignited within Kiran. Perhaps there was a way to wield the sword's power without sacrificing her own life force. Perhaps within this hidden grove lay the key to unlocking the weapon's true potential.

The next morning, she shared her discovery with Raju. His brow furrowed in concern. "The Whispering Woods," he muttered, his voice laced with apprehension. "A place of legends and myths, shrouded in mist and rumored to be guarded by unseen dangers."

Kiran understood his reservations. The Whispering Woods held an unsettling reputation amongst the villagers. Stories spoke of strange occurrences, of travelers who entered and never returned, and of a malevolent presence that lurked within its depths.

But the potential reward outweighed the risk. Kiran wouldn't back down. "We can't face the Blight again without every advantage at our disposal," she declared, her voice firm with resolve. "The whispers speak of knowledge, Raju. Knowledge that could save us all."

Raju, seeing the unwavering determination in her eyes, knew he couldn't dissuade her. With a resigned sigh, he agreed to accompany her. Together, they embarked on a perilous journey into the heart of the Whispering Woods.

The forest floor, unlike the familiar woods surrounding the village, was carpeted with a thick layer of damp, decaying leaves. Sunlight struggled to penetrate the dense canopy overhead, casting the woods in an eerie twilight. The air hung heavy with an oppressive silence, broken only by the occasional rustle of unseen creatures and the unsettling creak of ancient branches swaying in the nonexistent breeze.

As they ventured deeper, the whispers on the wind intensified, morphing from comforting guides into a cacophony of unsettling voices. They spoke of forgotten names, whispered secrets, and chilling warnings that sent shivers down Kiran's spine.

The path ahead grew treacherous. Thorny vines snagged at their clothes, and gnarled roots twisted underfoot, threatening to trip them at every turn. The oppressive silence was punctuated by the unsettling chirping of unseen insects and the unsettling feeling of being watched. Doubt gnawed at Kiran's resolve. Was this a fool's errand? Had they been misled by the whispers?

Just as despair threatened to engulf them, they stumbled upon a clearing bathed in an ethereal glow. In the center stood a grove of ancient trees, their branches intertwined to form a natural canopy overhead. The air within the grove hummed with an otherworldly energy, a stark contrast to the oppressive atmosphere of the surrounding woods.

This, Kiran knew instinctively, was the place the whispers had guided them towards. Relief washed over her, momentarily erasing the gnawing fear that had taken root in her heart.

As Kiran and Raju stepped into the clearing, the whispers on the wind morphed into a single, melodic voice. It resonated deep within their minds, a voice both ancient and wise.

"Welcome, children of nature," the voice boomed, echoing through the grove. "You who seek knowledge, you who stand defiant against the Blight."

Kiran looked around, searching for the source of the voice, but the ancient trees stood silent, their branches swaying gently in the nonexistent breeze.

"Who are you?" Raju called out, his voice cautious.

"I am the guardian of this grove," the voice replied, "a keeper of forgotten lore and a witness to ages past."

Kiran stepped forward, her gaze fixed on the shimmering air before her. "We seek knowledge," she said, her voice ringing with conviction. "Knowledge of the starlit sword, of how to wield its power without sacrificing my own life force."

The grove remained silent for a moment, the only sound the gentle rustling of leaves. Then, the voice resumed, its tone laced with a hint of sadness.

"The starlit sword," it intoned, "is a weapon forged from the essence of a dying star, imbued with immense power but burdened with a heavy price. Its true potential lies not in brute force, but in harmony."

Kiran frowned. "Harmony?" she echoed, unsure what the voice meant.

"The sword," the voice explained, "is a conduit, a channel for the power that flows through all living things. To wield it effectively, you must learn to resonate with that power, to become one with the flow of life itself."

Raju, ever the pragmatist, scoffed. "That sounds like cryptic nonsense," he muttered.

The voice sighed, a sound like wind rustling through ancient leaves. "Perhaps," it conceded, "but it is nonetheless the truth. The starlit sword cannot be mastered through brute force alone. It requires a connection, a deep understanding of the very life force it seeks to channel."

Kiran pondered this new information. Harmony. It resonated with her, a key she hadn't considered before. The whispers on the wind, the pulsating life force of the wellspring – perhaps these were the keys to unlocking the true potential of the sword.

"How do we achieve this harmony?" she asked, her voice laced with eagerness.

"The grove itself holds the answer," the voice replied. "Within its depths lie trials and challenges, tests designed to forge a deeper connection with nature. Only by succeeding in these trials can you hope to unlock the true power of the starlit sword."

A shiver of anticipation ran down Kiran's spine. Trials? Challenges? This was more than she had bargained for, but the alternative, facing the Blight with only a fraction of the sword's power, was far more terrifying.

"We are willing," she declared, her voice unwavering. "We will face your trials."

The voice seemed to hum with satisfaction. "Very well then," it echoed. "Let your journey begin."

As Kiran and Raju stood in the center of the grove, a shimmering portal materialized before them, swirling with vibrant colors. The whispers on the wind intensified, urging them forward. This was the point of no return.

Raju, his face etched with apprehension, looked at Kiran. "Are you sure this is wise?" he asked.

Kiran met his gaze, her eyes filled with determination. "We have no choice," she said. "The fate of our world depends on it."

Taking a deep breath, she stepped forward, the shimmering portal engulfing her in its light. With a final questioning look at Kiran, Raju followed suit, disappearing into the swirling vortex.

The portal shimmered and faded, leaving the grove bathed in an ethereal silence. The trials had begun, and the fate of the starlit sword, and perhaps the world itself, rested on the shoulders of Kiran and Raju venturing into the unknown.

Deep within the heart of the grove, hidden from sight, a pair of ancient eyes gleamed with a faint amusement. The trials designed to forge harmony were not without their dangers, but they were also filled with potential. It had been a long time since anyone had dared to face them, and the guardian of the grove was curious to see how these young champions would fare. Perhaps, just perhaps, they might hold the key to finally defeating the Blight and restoring balance to the world.

The first trial materialized before Kiran and Raju in a flash of blinding light. They found themselves standing on a rocky outcrop, surrounded by a churning vortex of wind. The wind howled with a fury that threatened to tear them from their precarious perch.

Kiran, her heart pounding in her chest, tightened her grip on the hilt of the starlit sword, a weapon she barely understood. Glancing at Raju, she saw a similar mix of fear and ...determination etched on his face.

"We have to stay calm," she shouted over the howling wind, her voice barely audible. "The whispers said harmony. We need to work with the wind, not fight it."

Raju nodded, his face grim. "Easier said than done," he yelled back, the wind whipping his words away.

Taking a deep breath, Kiran closed her eyes, focusing on the whispers that seemed to be carried on the very wind itself. It wasn't a soothing melody this time, but a chaotic symphony of howls, gusts, and eddies. Yet, within the chaos, Kiran began to sense a pattern, a rhythm to the wind's fury.

She imagined herself becoming part of the wind, her body flowing and bending with its every whim. Slowly, she started to move in sync with its chaotic dance. Her steps became lighter, her movements more fluid. The wind, sensing her willingness to cooperate, began to lessen its intensity, the howls morphing into a low hum.

"Raju, look!" she shouted, opening her eyes. She pointed to where the wind swirled around a central point, forming a shimmering vortex in the center of the storm.

Raju, following her gaze, saw what she meant. "That must be the way out," he yelled.

Carefully, Kiran moved towards the vortex, her steps light and graceful. Raju, emboldened by her success, followed suit. As they neared the swirling vortex, the wind seemed to guide them, pushing them gently towards the center.

With a final surge of energy, they leaped into the vortex. The world spun around them, a kaleidoscope of colors and wind-whipped landscapes. Then, just as abruptly as it began, the world solidified. They found themselves standing on a verdant patch of land, the fierce wind replaced by a gentle breeze.

They had passed the first trial. Relief washed over them, mixed with a newfound respect for the power and complexity of nature. The whispers on the wind, previously a source of guidance, now held a deeper meaning.

Their journey continued, leading them through a series of challenging landscapes. They navigated a scorching desert, learning to withstand the sun's blistering heat and coaxing life-giving water from parched earth. They traversed a frozen wasteland, forging a connection with the chilling embrace of winter and manipulating the flow of ice and snow.

Each trial pushed them to their limits, both physically and mentally. But with each challenge they conquered, their connection to nature deepened. They learned to understand the whispers, not just as sounds, but as a language of life itself, a symphony of interconnected forces.

One trial, however, stood out from the rest. Deep within a cavern, bathed in an eerie green glow, they encountered a twisted, monstrous version of the Blight. This creature, seemingly born from the very essence of darkness, embodied the destructive potential of nature if left unchecked.

Fear threatened to consume Kiran. This monstrous entity felt far more real, far more dangerous than the Blight creatures they had faced before. But the whispers, stronger than ever, urged her forward.

This wasn't a fight to be won with brute force. This was a test of their understanding of harmony. The whispers spoke of balancing the light within the darkness, of recognizing the inherent duality in nature.

Drawing on her newfound connection to life force, Kiran focused on channeling not just raw power, but also a sense of calm, of serenity. She surrounded the monstrous creature with a shimmering blue light, a counterpoint to its sickly green aura.

The creature recoiled, its form flickering and unsettling as the light washed over it. It wasn't being vanquished; it was being soothed, its destructive tendencies calmed by the touch of harmony.

As the light intensified, the monstrous creature began to morph, its twisted form reshaping into a beautiful, ethereal creature of pure energy. It pulsed with a vibrant light, a reflection of the harmony Kiran had channeled.

This was the true form of the Blight, not a mindless force of destruction, but an entity yearning for balance. It had been corrupted by something, twisted by an unknown force.

The whispers, clear and poignant, filled Kiran's mind. "The Blight is not your enemy," they echoed. "It is a mirror, reflecting the imbalance within your world."

Kiran understood. The Blight, in a way, was a symptom of a deeper problem, a world teetering on the edge of destruction. Their fight wasn't just against the Blight itself, but against the forces that had corrupted it.

With a newfound purpose, Kiran and Raju emerged from the caverns. The trials had transformed them. They weren't just warriors; they were guardians, entrusted with the responsibility of maintaining the delicate balance of nature.

But their journey wasn't over. The whispers spoke of another entity, a hidden darkness lurking beyond the tear in the sky, the true source of the Blight's corruption. This final confrontation, the whispers warned, would test their newfound connection to nature to its very core.

Back in the clearing, the guardian of the grove awaited them, its ancient eyes gleaming with a newfound respect. "You have done well," it boomed, its voice echoing through the grove. "You have faced your challenges and emerged stronger, more attuned to the rhythm of life."

Kiran and Raju looked at each other, a silent understanding passing between them. They had faced their fears, delved deep into the essence of nature, and emerged transformed. However, the fight ahead loomed large.

"The whispers spoke of a greater threat," Kiran said, her voice firm despite the tremor in her heart. "A darkness beyond the tear."

The guardian's ethereal form shimmered. "Indeed," it replied. "The true master of the Blight, a force fueled by chaos and destruction."

"How do we defeat it?" Raju asked, his voice laced with urgency. "We can't face another enemy like the one we encountered in the cave."

"This final confrontation will require a different approach," the guardian explained. "It will require not just strength, but a unified force of nature, a symphony of light and life to counter the encroaching darkness."

Kiran understood. The trials had taught them about harmony, about working with nature, not against it. Defeating this ultimate darkness wouldn't be achieved through brute force, but through a collective effort, a testament to the interconnectedness of all living things.

"We can gather the villagers," she declared, her voice ringing with newfound resolve. "Together, we can channel the very essence of life, a force that cannot be extinguished."

The guardian nodded approvingly. "Time is of the essence," it warned. "The darkness grows stronger with each passing day. You must act swiftly."

With a newfound sense of purpose, Kiran and Raju retraced their steps back to the village. The whispering woods, once a place of unease, now held a sense of respect. They had ventured within its depths, faced its trials, and emerged stronger, forever bound to the rhythm of life.

Back in the village, Kiran addressed the gathered people, her voice resonating with the echoes of the whispers. She spoke of their journey, of the trials they had faced, and the true nature of the Blight. More importantly, she spoke of hope, of a collective force they could muster, a symphony of nature that could push back the encroaching darkness.

The villagers, their faces filled with trepidation but also a flicker of resolve, listened intently. They knew the stakes were higher than ever before. This was the final battle, the line in the sand between light and darkness.

Under Kiran's guidance, the villagers gathered their resources. They chanted ancient songs passed down through generations, songs that spoke of unity and balance. They channeled the power of the wellspring, its life-giving essence resonating through their veins.

As the tear in the sky pulsed ominously, casting an unsettling shadow over the village, Kiran raised the starlit sword. The whispers flowed through her, a torrent of life force channeling through the blade. The sword, bathed in an ethereal glow, hummed with a power unlike anything they had ever witnessed.

The villagers, responding to Kiran's call, unleashed a collective surge of energy. The wind howled with a fury fueled by purpose, the earth trembled with a renewed strength, and the water coalesced into a shimmering shield, a barrier against the encroaching darkness.

A monstrous entity, a swirling vortex of pure chaos, emerged from the tear. This was the true mastermind, the ultimate source of the Blight's corruption. It reached towards the village, its tendrils seeking to extinguish the flickering flame of life.

But the villagers stood firm. Kiran, channeling the whispers and the collective energy, swung the starlit sword. A wave of light, imbued with the symphony of nature's power, surged forth, clashing with the entity's dark tendrils.

The air crackled with energy, the ground trembling from the force of the collision. Light and darkness battled in a dazzling display of power, a struggle for the very soul of their world.

Kiran, her heart pounding in her chest, held her ground. She knew this was her fight, the culmination of her journey. With one final, desperate surge of energy, she channeled the very essence of life into the starlit sword.

The blade pulsed with an intensity that rivaled a star going supernova. The light engulfed the entity, pushing it back further and further into the tear. Then, with a deafening roar, the tear slammed shut, sealing the darkness within.

Silence descended upon the village. The villagers, exhausted but exhilarated, watched in disbelief as the tear in the sky vanished, leaving behind a clear

Chapter 6: Whispers of a Shadow

The air hung heavy with the aftermath of battle. Jubilation mingled with exhaustion in the village square. Cheers and relieved laughter echoed through the cobbled streets, a testament to their hard-won victory. Yet, beneath the surface, a sliver of unease gnawed at Kiran. The tear in the sky was sealed, but the whispers on the wind, now faint and fragmented, carried a chilling warning. The darkness was contained, not destroyed.

Days bled into weeks as the villagers set about rebuilding. Homes shattered by the Blight's onslaught were mended, fields lay fallow but held the promise of renewed life, and a collective sigh of relief seemed to permeate the air. Yet, Kiran couldn't shake the gnawing feeling that their respite was temporary, a pause before the storm.

One starlit night, as she stood vigil under the banyan tree, the familiar whispers returned, stronger this time, but laced with an unsettling urgency. They spoke of a shadow lurking beyond the sealed tear, a malevolent entity writhing in its confinement, plotting its return.

The whispers revealed a chilling truth – the entity that orchestrated the Blight wasn't a mindless force, but a being of immense power and cunning. It thrived on discord and imbalance, and the tear, though sealed, wasn't an impenetrable barrier. Left unchecked, it would weaken with time, allowing the entity to push its tendrils through, poisoning the world once more.

Kiran's heart sank. Their victory felt bittersweet. They had won the battle, but the war was far from over. Despair threatened to consume her, but the whispers urged her forward. They spoke of a hidden knowledge, a forgotten power that could permanently sever the entity's connection to their world.

But this knowledge resided deep within the Whispering Woods, a place even more dangerous now with the entity's rage simmering on the other side of the tear. Fear gnawed at Kiran, but the weight of responsibility rested heavily on her shoulders. If the whispers were right, venturing into the woods was the only option, a perilous journey to seek a weapon against a shadow they couldn't even see.

The next morning, Kiran stood before the village elders, her face a mask of resolve. She shared the whispers' chilling message, the knowledge of a looming threat. The silence in the council chamber was heavy, broken only by the rasp of worried breaths.

Elder Kaia, her weathered face etched with concern, spoke first. "The Whispering Woods," she rasped, "a place fraught with danger even in times of peace. To venture within now, with the entity stirring..."

Kiran understood their apprehension. Yet, she had to try. "We cannot afford to wait," she declared, her voice ringing with conviction. "The longer we delay, the stronger the entity becomes. There must be a way to permanently sever its hold on our world."

Raju, ever the pragmatist, stepped forward. "But who would undertake such a perilous journey?" he asked.

Kiran met his gaze, her eyes blazing with determination. "I will," she said, her voice unwavering. "The whispers first spoke to me, and they may hold the key to finding this hidden knowledge. But I won't go alone."

She scanned the anxious faces of the villagers, her gaze finally settling on a young hunter named Rohan. His eyes, once filled with the fiery intensity of his flames, mirrored her own resolve. He understood the risk, the weight of responsibility, but also the necessity.

With a stoic nod, Rohan stepped forward, a flicker of determination lighting his eyes. "I'll go with you, Kiran. We faced the Blight together, and we can face this unknown danger as well."

Kiran smiled, a flicker of warmth chasing away the shadows of fear. Together, they would venture into the heart of the Whispering Woods, a place where the whispers grew louder and the shadows stretched longer. Their journey, fraught with danger and uncertainty, would decide the fate of their world, hanging precariously in the balance between the whispers of a forgotten power and the looming shadow of a lurking darkness.

Chapter 7: Echoes in the Gloom

The familiar path leading into the Whispering Woods seemed to have contorted under the weight of the sealed tear. Sunlight, once dappled and playful, struggled to penetrate the dense canopy, casting the forest floor in an unsettling gloom. The air, thick and heavy, hung stagnant, devoid of the chirping of insects or the rustling of leaves. An oppressive silence reigned, broken only by the unsettling crunch of dead leaves under their boots and the erratic thumping of Kiran's heart.

Kiran, her hand gripping the hilt of the starlit sword, felt a tremor of unease run down her spine. The whispers, once a comforting guide, now crackled with a chilling urgency, a distorted symphony of warnings and fragmented visions.

Rohan, his face etched with a mixture of apprehension and determination, walked a pace behind her. His trusty bow, strung with an arrow imbued with the wellspring's essence, was his only solace in this unsettling environment.

As they ventured deeper, the whispers intensified, morphing into a cacophony of unsettling voices. They spoke of twisted creatures guarding forgotten secrets, of shadows that clung to the very fabric of reality, and of a maddening silence that promised oblivion.

Suddenly, the path ahead vanished, swallowed by a thick wall of thorny vines. The whispers, for a fleeting moment, coalesced into a single, chilling voice, "Welcome...fools."

Kiran exchanged a worried glance with Rohan. Fear threatened to paralyze her, but the weight of their responsibility propelled her forward. Taking a deep breath, she channeled the whispers, focusing on the underlying rhythm, the melody beneath the chaos.

A vision flickered in her mind – a hidden passage veiled by a tapestry of vines, pulsating with a faint, ethereal glow. With newfound certainty, she guided Rohan towards the seemingly impenetrable wall.

Following her instructions, Rohan, with nimble fingers, began to untangle the thorny mass. Slowly, painstakingly, they revealed a narrow passage, barely wide enough for a single person to squeeze through.

"I'll go first," Kiran declared, her voice tight with apprehension.

Rohan nodded, his hand lingering on her shoulder for a moment, a silent gesture of support. With a final deep breath, Kiran stepped into the inky blackness of the passage.

The air inside was thick and suffocating, the silence broken only by the rhythmic thud of her own heartbeat. The whispers, once a cacophony, had vanished, replaced by an unsettling emptiness. Kiran fumbled for her flint and tinder, the meager flame a beacon of hope in the suffocating darkness.

The passage twisted and turned, a labyrinth carved into the very heart of the woods. Each step forward felt like a descent into the unknown. Just as doubt began to gnaw at her resolve, the faint glow from Kiran's vision emerged ahead, beckoning her forward.

The passage opened into a hidden cavern, bathed in an ethereal, bioluminescent light emanating from strange, pulsating fungi clinging to the cavern walls. In the center stood a gnarled, ancient tree, its branches reaching out like skeletal fingers, its bark etched with symbols that seemed to writhe and pulsate in the otherworldly light.

As Kiran approached the tree, the whispers returned, a chorus of fragmented knowledge echoing within her mind. The symbols on the bark, they revealed, were not mere decoration but a map, a guide to a hidden wellspring of power, a reservoir of forgotten magic capable of severing the entity's connection to their world.

But the whispers also warned of a guardian, a creature born from the darkness itself, tasked with protecting this hidden knowledge. A tremor of fear ran down Kiran's spine, the silence in the cavern broken only by the rasping sound of her own breath.

Suddenly, the shadows at the edge of the cavern writhed and coalesced, forming a monstrous creature – a grotesque amalgamation of Blight creatures they had faced before, its eyes burning with an unholy light.

This was the guardian, a physical manifestation of the entity's rage and corruption. Kiran knew they couldn't avoid a fight. With a determined glint in her eyes, she drew the starlit sword, its blade humming with a faint blue light, a beacon of hope against the encroaching darkness.

Rohan, ever vigilant, nocked an arrow imbued with the wellspring's essence onto his bowstring. The cavern echoed with a silent challenge as Kiran and Rohan braced themselves for a fight unlike any they had faced before. The fate of their world hinged on their success, on their ability to defeat the guardian and claim the power hidden within the ancient tree, a desperate gamble against a shadow that lurked just beyond the sealed tear.

Lessons and Uniqueness of the Story

L essons Learned:

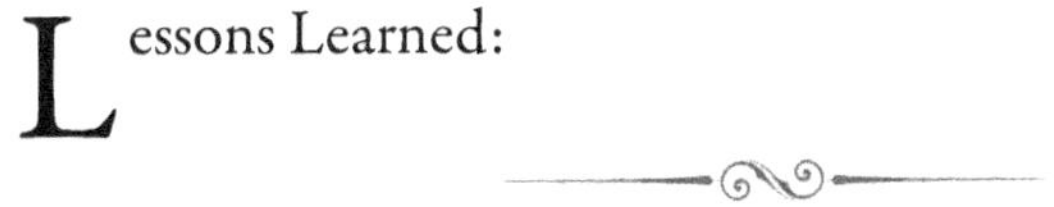

POWER OF UNITY AND Collaboration: The characters of Kiran and Rohan showcase how friendship and collaboration can overcome daunting challenges.

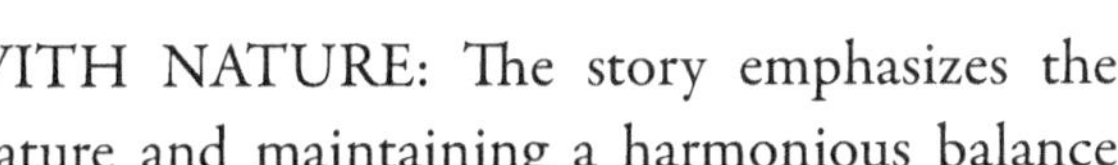

HARMONY WITH NATURE: The story emphasizes the importance of nature and maintaining a harmonious balance with it.

HOPE AND DETERMINATION: Kiran and Rohan embody how hope and unwavering determination can help achieve seemingly impossible goals.

INNER STRENGTH: KIRAN'S character represents how our inner strength and potential can empower us to face unimaginable challenges.

Unique Aspects:

Blending Language and Nature: The story skillfully weaves poetic language with elements of nature, creating an immersive experience for readers.

Moral and Environmental Message: The narrative subtly integrates moral and environmental messages, prompting readers to contemplate their responsibility towards nature.

MYSTERY AND THE UNKNOWN: The story utilizes elements of mystery and the unknown to keep readers engaged and curious about what unfolds next.

CHARACTER DEVELOPMENT: Kiran and Rohan undergo significant development throughout the narrative, making them more relatable and inspiring.

CONCLUSION:

This story not only entertains but also imparts valuable life lessons to its readers. It highlights the importance of nature, cooperation, and hope, inspiring readers to make positive changes in their own lives.

About the Author

Mrigendra Bharti, born on June 29, 2004, in South Delhi, India, is a multifaceted individual recognized as the owner of Mrigendra Bharti Group InfoTech India Co. Pvt Ltd. Beyond his entrepreneurial endeavors, he is a distinguished music producer, director, and a budding writer.

Embarking on his professional journey at a young age, Mrigendra Bharti's visionary leadership has led to the establishment of several successful ventures, including Croma Music Series Entertainment, Sellbrochure, Fauget Innovative, and more.

What sets Mrigendra apart is his early initiation into the world of business. His foray into the unknown realms of entrepreneurship began during his 10th-grade years, where he delved into the music industry. This initial venture laid the foundation for subsequent achievements, showcasing his dedication and resilience.

Having honed his skills in music, Mrigendra Bharti not only demonstrated significant growth in his craft but also expanded his professional network. His passion extends beyond music, encompassing app and website development, as well as graphic design.

Fueled by his creative aspirations, Mrigendra established the Mrigendra Bharti Group, a company specializing in website and app development. Currently, he collaborates with a dedicated team, collectively working on ambitious projects that promise innovation and excellence.

Mrigendra's journey serves as an inspiration, particularly for today's students, highlighting the potential of youthful determination and the ability to transform innovative ideas into successful businesses. As he continues to make strides in various domains, Mrigendra Bharti remains a dynamic force, contributing vibrancy to the realms of business, music, and technology.

Read more at https://www.imwriter-mrigendra.rf.gd.